D1400423

SAHASRA
VURAY

AMELIA BEDELIA'S
BACKPACK BUNDLE

BY Herman Parish PICTURES BY Lynn Sweat

Greenwillow Books
An Imprint of HarperCollinsPublishers

This 2012 edition licensed for publication by Sandy Creek by HarperCollins Publishers.
SANDY CREEK and the distinctive Sandy Creek logo are trademarks of Barnes and Noble, Inc.

An Imprint of Sterling Publishing
387 Park Avenue South
New York, NY 10016

Amelia Bedelia, Bookworm
© 2003 by HERMAN S. PARISH III
Illustrations © 2003 by LYNN SWEAT

Amelia Bedelia, Rocket Scientist?
© 2005 by HERMAN S. PARISH III
Illustrations © 2005 by LYNN SWEAT

Amelia Bedelia's Masterpiece
© 2007 by HERMAN S. PARISH III
Illustrations © 2007 by LYNN SWEAT

Amelia Bedelia is a registered trademark of Peppermint Partners, LLC.
Watercolors and a black pen were used for the full-color art.
The text type is Times.

Greenwillow Books

All rights reserved. No part of this publication may be reproduced, stored in a retrieval system, or
transmitted, in any form or by any means, electronic, mechanical, photocopying, recording, or
otherwise, without prior written permission from the publisher.

ISBN 978-1-4351-4392-0

HarperCollins ISBN: 978-0-06-223091-1

Amelia Bedelia, Bookworm Library of Congress Cataloging-in-Publication Data: 2002035329
Amelia Bedelia, Rocket Scientist? Library of Congress Cataloging-in-Publication Data: 2004011830
Amelia Bedelia's Masterpiece Library of Congress Cataloging-in-Publication Data: 2006020010

For information about custom editions, special sales, and premium and corporate purchases, please con-
tact Sterling Special Sales at 800-805-5489 or specialsales@sterlingpublishing.com.

Manufactured in China
Lot #:
12 13 14 15 16 SCP 10 9 8 7 6 5 4 3 2 1

Manufactured 06/12

AMELIA BEDELIA'S
BACKPACK BUNDLE

BY Herman Parish PICTURES BY Lynn Sweat

TABLE OF CONTENTS

AMELIA BEDELIA'S MASTERPIECE

BY HERMAN PARISH

PICTURES BY LYNN SWEAT

For my pal Jay Jasper
—H. P.

To Elynor
—L. S.

The minute Amelia Bedelia

walked into the art museum,

she knew it would be an exciting day.

"Wow," said Amelia Bedelia.

"Look at all of this amazing art.

The people look interesting, too."

One person stood out from the others.

Everyone was staring at him.

"It is not polite to stare,"

said Amelia Bedelia.

"I will make him feel at home."

She walked over to the man and said,

"Excuse me. What are you looking at?"

He did not answer, so she said,

"It must be very interesting."

He didn't say a word, so she said,

"May I borrow your binoculars?"

He did not move a muscle.

"I will get his attention," said Amelia Bedelia.

She reached out to tap him on the shoulder.

Suddenly, a voice behind her boomed out.

"Do not touch the art!"

"Yipes!" said Amelia Bedelia.

She jumped behind the man and hid.

"Mrs. Rogers!" said Amelia Bedelia.

"You scared the daylights out of me."

"I am so sorry," said Mrs. Rogers.

"You are not allowed to touch the art."

"Is his name Art?" said Amelia Bedelia.

"No, he . . . it . . . is art," said Mrs. Rogers.

"It is a sculpture called *Birdwatcher*."

"The artist fooled me," said Amelia Bedelia.

"It's tough to tell the people from the art."

"Come along," said Mrs. Rogers.

"Let me show you some other works of art."

They walked across the main gallery.

"Thanks for coming," said Mrs. Rogers.

"The museum needs your help today."

"My pleasure," said Amelia Bedelia.

"It's fun to be surrounded by art."

"This isn't the art," said Mrs. Rogers.

"This is the museum gift shop."

"This is a store?" said Amelia Bedelia.

"You mean this stuff is for sale?"

"Oh my, yes," said Mrs. Rogers.

"These are genuine reproductions."

"I get it," said Amelia Bedelia.

"These are real fakes."

"I guess so," said Mrs. Rogers.

"That is one way to put it."

Amelia Bedelia saw a familiar face

staring at her from a shelf.

"Look here," said Amelia Bedelia.

"Who does this remind you of?"

"It's Cousin Alcolu!"

said Mrs. Rogers.

"Were his ancestors Roman?"

"They sure were," said Amelia Bedelia.

"His family was roaming all over

  the United States."

"I see," said Mrs. Rogers, with a laugh.

"Let's buy it for his birthday."

"How much is it?" said Amelia Bedelia.

"It is a bargain," said Mrs. Rogers.

"The real thing would be priceless."

"Price less?" said Amelia Bedelia.

"Without a price, it would be free."

"Not really," said Mrs. Rogers.

"Compared to the original art,

  this reproduction is worthless."

"Worth less?" said Amelia Bedelia.

"Worth less than what?"

"Than the real thing," said Mrs. Rogers.

"That sounds wacky," said Amelia Bedelia.

"If the real thing doesn't have a price,

how could it be worth more?"

Just then, a man walked up to them.

"Amelia Bedelia," said Mrs. Rogers,

"meet the director of the museum."

"Pleased to meet you," the director said.

"My name is Arthur Stiles,

but you can call me Art."

"Nice to meet you," said Amelia Bedelia.

"You have been very busy, Art.

This museum is full of works of Art."

Art laughed and said,

"I wish I were that talented.

I take care of the art collection.

I can't take credit for it."

"I'm a collector, too,"

said Amelia Bedelia.

"Of what?" said Art.

"Paintings? Sculptures?"

"Aluminum foil," said Amelia Bedelia.

She reached in her purse

and pulled out a big shiny ball of foil.

"She's very handy," said Mrs. Rogers,

"and she's our newest volunteer."

"That is terrific," said Art.

"You could work here in the store."

"Great," said Amelia Bedelia.

"With my employee discount,

I will save Mrs. Rogers lots of money."

"Amelia Bedelia!" said Mrs. Rogers.

"Do not be so forward."

Amelia Bedelia took a step backward.

"If you think about discounts," said Art,

"you must have a head for figures."

"Really?" said Amelia Bedelia.

"I have an idea," said Art.

"Look around the museum.

See what interests you.

Then we can figure out

a way for you to help."

"Sounds like a plan," said Amelia Bedelia.

"Before I go,

may I buy this?"

"Certainly,"

said Art.

"I will even give you

my discount on that bust."

"Bust?" asked Amelia Bedelia.

"Is it a bargain because

it's busted?"

"It isn't broken," said Mrs. Rogers.

"Of course not," said Art.

"A 'bust' is a sculpture of the head,

shoulders, and chest."

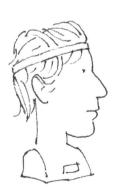

"I see," said Amelia Bedelia.

"You can see the real thing," said Art,

"if you walk through that door."

Amelia Bedelia said thanks and good-bye.

Then she took the shopping bag

and headed off to explore.

Amelia Bedelia found the real bust right away.

"Oh my gosh," said Amelia Bedelia.

"Here is Cousin Alcolu, just like Art said.

And there is no price on it,

just like Mrs. Rogers said."

Amelia Bedelia took the bust

out of her bag.

She unwrapped it and compared it

to the one on the pedestal.

"The bust we bought is in better shape.

I know how to help the museum.

I will loan the museum our bust

while I take the price less one home

and clean it up."

Amelia Bedelia swapped the busts.

She carefully wrapped

the museum bust,

put it in her bag, and tidied up.

"Ah-CHOO!" Amelia Bedelia sneezed.

"Ancient art is so musty and dusty.

Maybe I should try something newer."

THIS WAY
TO MODERN
ART →

Amelia Bedelia saw a sign.

She did exactly what it said.

"I see why they called this one

Banana Split. It sure is!"

27

"Ouch!

This reminds me of the day

Mr. Rogers ran his car

into the garage door."

"Did they hang this one upside down?

I'll bet the floor was covered with paint.

Looks like somebody already cleaned it up."

When Amelia Bedelia turned the corner,

she was shocked by what she saw.

"My goodness," said Amelia Bedelia.

"Art would be mad to see this mess

in his museum.

I'll straighten it up right now."

Amelia Bedelia got the cleaning cart

from the other gallery and went to work.

"How strange," said Amelia Bedelia.

"All of the food is plastic.

No wonder they left it behind."

Amelia Bedelia worked as fast as she could.

She finished up

just as Art walked into the gallery.

"Here you are," said Art.

"What have you been up to?"

"See for yourself," said Amelia Bedelia.

Art couldn't believe his eyes.

"Amelia Bedelia!" shouted Art.

"What have you done?"

"I cleaned up," said Amelia Bedelia.

"I am a housekeeper.

I know exactly what I'm doing."

"It wasn't a mess," said Art.

"This was a work of art."

"Please," said Amelia Bedelia.

"Don't blame yourself, Art.

This was the work of a slob."

"No, it wasn't," said Art.

"A famous modern artist

installed this work of art.

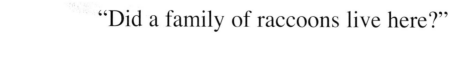

She called it *Family Room*."

"Whose family?" said Amelia Bedelia.

"Did a family of raccoons live here?"

"We disagree about art," said Art.

"But if you keep helping like this,

we won't have a museum left.

Do not touch one more thing! Please!"

Art walked away, shaking his head.

Amelia Bedelia felt terrible.

A teacher with students passed by

on a tour of the museum.

Amelia Bedelia decided to follow them.

In the next gallery, the students

gathered around their teacher.

"What type of painting is this?"

asked the teacher.

"It's a landscape,"

said a boy.

"And what kind of painting is this?"

she asked.

"That's a seascape," said a girl.

"And what is this?" the teacher asked.

Amelia Bedelia raised her hand.

"I know," she said. "It's a fire escape."

All the children laughed and giggled.

One of the students said, "It's a cityscape."

"That figures," said Amelia Bedelia.

"Are you Amelia Bedelia?"

asked the teacher.

"That's me," said Amelia Bedelia.

"I thought so," said the teacher.

"You helped at our school play last year."

"That was fun," said Amelia Bedelia.

"May I ask a favor?" said the teacher.

"One of my students doesn't feel well.

Would you please sit with him

until we complete our tour?"

"I'd be glad to," said Amelia Bedelia.

A boy with a sketchpad came forward.

"He is the best artist in our school,"

said the teacher. "His name is Drew."

"You'll fit right in," said Amelia Bedelia.

"The head of the museum is named Art."

The class moved on.

Drew began to draw.

"How do you feel?" asked Amelia Bedelia.

"Much better," said Drew.

"I was sick of hearing about art.

I want to *do* art."

"What do you like to draw best?"

asked Amelia Bedelia.

"I like figures," said Drew.

"Me, too," said Amelia Bedelia.

"My favorite is the number eight."

"Not number figures," said Drew.

"Human figures. People tell me

I have an eye for figures."

"That's funny," said Amelia Bedelia.

"I was told I have a head for figures."

"Well," said Drew. "Let's go figure."

They laughed and walked next door.

"Shhhh," said Drew. "A real artist."

"He must work for the museum,"

whispered Amelia Bedelia,

"making genuine reproductions."

"Maybe not," said Drew.

"Many artists copy famous paintings

to improve their skills."

They watched him paint some more.

"He is very talented," said Drew.

"He sure is," said Amelia Bedelia.

"I can't tell his copy from the real thing."

Another kind of painter walked by.

"Golly," said Amelia Bedelia.

"This place is full of painters."

They followed him into an empty gallery.

"Where are the paintings?"

asked Drew.

"You just missed them,"

said the painter.

"I repaint the walls

after an exhibit is over."

"Hey, I have an idea,"

 said Amelia Bedelia.

"If you're going to

 paint over these walls,

 could Drew draw on them now, for fun?"

"Sure," said the painter. "Why not?

 He can borrow my paints and brushes.

 I won't need them until after lunch."

 The painter sat down to eat a sandwich.

"Try my brush," said Amelia Bedelia.

"I'll go see if that other painter

 has finished his masterpiece."

"See you later," said Drew.

"Look at that," said Amelia Bedelia.

"He replaced that old painting with his new one.

I'll bet he wants to take it home to clean it up."

The painter took the painting away.

"Good," said Amelia Bedelia.

"I can look without bothering him."

When she leaned forward,

some paint got on her bonnet.

"Uh-oh," said Amelia Bedelia.

"This paint is still wet."

Amelia Bedelia had a good idea.

She took out her ball of foil.

She used some foil

to cover the wet parts.

"That's better,"

said Amelia Bedelia.

"Folks won't get paint on themselves."

She went back to check on Drew.

Incredible figures covered the walls.

"Drew," said Amelia Bedelia.

"Way to go! This looks great."

"Thanks a lot," said Drew.

"I've never had so much fun!"

"Wow," said the painter.

"That kid is painting up a storm."

"No," said Amelia Bedelia.

"He paints figures, not weather."

Amelia Bedelia asked the painter,

"May I borrow your Wet Paint sign?

A painting next door is wet."

"That's impossible," said the painter.

"Those paintings have been dry

for years."

"Sure," said Amelia Bedelia.

"The original art is dry,

but the genuine

reproduction is wet."

"What? Show me!"

said the painter.

Along the way, they met a security guard.

Amelia Bedelia told him what she had seen.

The guard called the director on his radio.

"Think back, lady," said the guard.

"Did you see any sketchy characters?"

"Just one man," said Amelia Bedelia.

"He wasn't sketching,

he was painting."

Art ran into the gallery.

"Amelia Bedelia," said Art.

"*Now* what have you done?"

WET
PAINT

"I did you a favor," said Amelia Bedelia.

"Now people won't get

wet paint on themselves."

Art tore off the foil

and touched the painting.

"Don't touch!" said Amelia Bedelia.

"Mrs. Rogers will yell at you."

Art saw wet paint on his finger.

"A forgery!" he shouted.

"We've been robbed—sound the alarm!"

A report came over the radio.

"Painting has been found.

Suspect surrounded.

All guards to Roman gallery."

Everyone ran to the Roman gallery.

"Stand back!"

screamed the thief.

"Or I will smash this to bits!"

"Do what he says," said Art.

"That bust is priceless."

"No, it isn't," said Amelia Bedelia.

"Go ahead and break it if you like."

"Catch!" said the thief.

He tossed the bust into the air.

As everyone tried to grab it,

the thief made his getaway.

CRASH!

The guards raced after the thief.

"Close all the doors," ordered Art.

"He can't escape."

Art picked up the pieces of the bust.

"Amelia Bedelia!

Why did you tell him that?

This bust was priceless."

"Nope," said Amelia Bedelia.

"Here is the one without a price."

She pulled the bust out of her bag.

"The real bust!" said Art.

"You swiped it and saved it."

"I didn't swipe it," said Amelia Bedelia.

"I swapped it."

A guard ran up holding the disguise.

"I guess he got away," he said.

"Keep searching," said Art,

"and keep me posted.

Thank you, Amelia Bedelia.

You saved a priceless work of art

and foiled a forgery.

How can we ever repay you?"

"For starters,"

said Amelia Bedelia,

"how about a new bust

for Cousin Alcolu?"

"Done!" said Art.

"Anything else?"

"Follow me," Amelia Bedelia said.

"My head for figures tells me

that you will like

what you see."

She led Art to Drew.

Art was stunned.

"Did you draw this?"

he asked the painter.

"Not me," said the painter.

"That kid, Drew."

"What is his name?" said Art.

"That's it," said Amelia Bedelia.

"You are Art. He is Drew."

"Did someone call me?" asked Drew.

"I did, young man," said Art.

"I am the director of this museum.

Did you draw on my walls?"

"Yes, I did," said Drew.

"The painter said it would be okay."

"I don't call this okay," said Art.

"I call it fabulous!"

"You do?" said Drew.

"Absolutely," said Art.

"These figures are spectacular.

Your drawings will be our next show."

Drew hugged Amelia Bedelia.

"Drew," she said, "you are a true artist."

When Drew's class heard the news,

they all clapped and cheered.

"How exciting," said the teacher.

"This calls for another field trip

to see what Drew has drawn."

Amelia Bedelia walked back

to the museum entrance

to meet Mrs. Rogers

and head for home.

The museum was almost empty.

"For goodness' sake," said Amelia Bedelia.

"That artist has made another sculpture.

I'll brush off the fuzz stuck on its nose."

She took out her duster and . . .

AHH-
CHOO!

"You are not an art work,"

said Amelia Bedelia.

"You must be the art thief!"

The man dropped to his knees.

"Please don't turn me in," he said.

"Shame on you," said Amelia Bedelia.

"You have talent and so much to give.

How could you think about taking?"

The thief's eyes filled with tears.

"You are right," said the thief.

"I am sorry. I won't steal ever again."

"Promise?" she asked.

"I promise," he said.

"I believe you," said Amelia Bedelia.

"And I believe in you. Now good-bye."

He thanked her and vanished.

A moment later, Mrs. Rogers showed up.

"Who was that man?" she asked.

"Just some guy," said Amelia Bedelia.

"He likes to stand around in art museums."

"You see?" said Mrs. Rogers.

"You meet the most interesting people here.

Did you hear about the attempted robbery?"

They had a lot to talk about on the way home.

The next month, the art museum

opened the exhibit of Drew's work.

Cousin Alcolu's birthday

was on the very same day.

"Congratulations, Drew," said Mrs. Rogers.

"The whole town is proud of you."

"Thank you so much," said Drew.

"The show is a big hit," said Mr. Rogers.

"Thank Amelia Bedelia," said Art.

"Here you are," said Amelia Bedelia.

As Cousin Alcolu served cake, he said,

"Every year, Amelia Bedelia bakes

a coconut cake for my birthday."

"Mmmm," said Art to Amelia Bedelia.

"This piece of cake is *your* masterpiece."

"Thank you," said Amelia Bedelia.

"Speaking of masterpieces,

here is your birthday present."

As Cousin Alcolu took it,

the gift slipped out of the bag.

"Oops!" said Cousin Alcolu.

"Not again," said Art.

"That was a bust," said Mrs. Rogers.

"It is now," said Mr. Rogers.

"It is in a million pieces."

"Don't worry," said Art.

"I know where to find another one."

"Thank you," said Amelia Bedelia.

"Just make sure it has a price."

"You can count on me," said Art.

"By the way, this came for you."

Amelia Bedelia unwrapped the package.

"This looks fantastic!" said Art.

"You've discovered another modern artist."

"Wow," said Drew. "Who did it?"

"There is a note," said Art.

Amelia Bedelia read it to herself.

"Turn around," said a man.

"I want to take your picture."

"No!" said Amelia Bedelia.

"You can't have it."

"Relax," said Art.

"He's a photographer."

Herman Parish

Amelia Bedelia, Bookworm

Pictures by Lynn Sweat

Greenwillow Books

An Imprint of HarperCollins*Publishers*

For Anne Bezverkov,
who loved books
—H. P.

For Elynor
—L. S.

"**H**i, Mrs. Page," said Amelia Bedelia.

"How is the world's best librarian?"

"Amelia Bedelia," said Mrs. Page.

"Am I glad to see you."

"I give up," said Amelia Bedelia.

"Are you glad to see me?"

"Of course I am," said Mrs. Page.

"I am just frazzled today."

"What's wrong?" said Amelia Bedelia.

"It is my boss," said Mrs. Page.

"The head librarian is stopping by.

When it comes to libraries and books,

she knows it all."

"She sounds very smart,"

said Amelia Bedelia.

"Did she invent books?"

"Almost," said Mrs. Page.

"She has been around forever."

"Don't worry," said Amelia Bedelia.

"She'll love your library. The children do."

"Thank you," said Mrs. Page.

"I just wish her visit could be special."

"I will help," said Amelia Bedelia.

"First, I must return some books."

Mrs. Page was astonished.

"What have you done to them?"

"Remember?" said Amelia Bedelia.

"You said these books needed jackets.

So I made a jacket for each one."

"This book got a sweater,"

said Mrs. Page.

"Sure," said Amelia Bedelia.

"It is about the North Pole.

It gets very cold there."

"Now I have seen everything,"

said Mrs. Page.

"This is one book

you *can* judge by its cover."

"Excuse me," said Mark.

"May I check out this book?"

"Certainly," said Mrs. Page.

"Here is your book, Mark."

"Yippee!" said Amelia Bedelia.

"Free bookmarks for everyone."

"Bookmarks?" said Mrs. Page.

"Who is giving out bookmarks?"

"You are," said a girl.

"You gave that boy a bookmark."

"I did not," said Mrs. Page.

"I said 'Here is your book, *Mark*,'

because that boy is named Mark."

"My name is Danny," said Danny.

"Too bad," said the girl.

"If you were named Mark,

   you could have a bookmark."

"That is not fair!" said Danny.

"Amelia Bedelia," said Mrs. Page,

"see what you have started?"

"I am sorry," said Amelia Bedelia.

Mrs. Page got paper, scissors, and pens.

"Children, Amelia Bedelia will help

each one of you to make a bookmark."

"What about Mark?" said Amelia Bedelia.

"Don't forget him," said Mrs. Page.

"Make him a bookmark, too.

Just be as quiet as you can.

I want to hear a pin drop."

"Okay," said Amelia Bedelia.

She threw her pen on the floor.

CLICK

"How was that?" said Amelia Bedelia.

"Do you want to hear my pen drop again?"

Mrs. Page shook her head and walked away.

Amelia Bedelia got right to work.

She drew a picture of Mark

on his bookmark.

She made each bookmark special.

"Next!" said Amelia Bedelia.

"What is your name?"

"My name is Ralph," the next boy said.

"But I don't need a bookmark.

 I need help with my school report."

"What is it about?" said Amelia Bedelia.

"Dinosaurs," he said. "You know,

brontosaurus, tyrannosaurus,

ste . . . stego . . ."

"Stego Saurus?" said Amelia Bedelia.

"That's the one," said Ralph.

"It figures," said Amelia Bedelia.

"If your last name is Saurus,

you are probably a dinosaur."

"Excuse me," said a girl.

"I need some help, too.

I am looking for a thesaurus."

"The Saurus?" said Amelia Bedelia.

"What kind of dinosaur is that?"

"I'm not sure," said the girl.

"Is a thesaurus a dinosaur?

My teacher said

I needed one to do my report."

"Gee," said Amelia Bedelia,

"you are way too late.

Every Saurus died

millions of years ago."

"What am I going to do now?"

said the girl.

"Let's make a bookmark for you,"

said Amelia Bedelia.

"What is your name?"

"My name is Lisa," she said.

"But I don't need a bookma[rk]

because Sam ate my book."

"Yipes!" said Amelia Bedelia.

"Is Sam okay? Where is he?"

"Sam is fine," said Lisa.

YIPES!

Lisa pointed out the window.

"Sam is cute," she said,

"but he chews up everything."

"Whew," said Amelia Bedelia.

"I was worried about Sam."

"I am worried, too," said Lisa.

"Mrs. Page will be mad

that her book got wrecked."

"I see," said Amelia Bedelia.

"Let's go talk with her."

"Mrs. Page," said Amelia Bedelia,

"Lisa has a book checked out."

Mrs. Page looked up the title.

"Here it is," said Mrs. Page.

"*How to Train Your Dog.*"

"That's the book," said Lisa.

"But Sam got it."

Mrs. Page corrected Lisa.

"You mean Sam *has* it.

Did he enjoy it?"

"He sure did," said Amelia Bedelia.

"Sam devoured it."

"Wonderful!" said Mrs. Page.

"We librarians love that."

"You do?" said Amelia Bedelia.

"Oh, yes," said Mrs. Page.

"But it breaks my heart

if a book is abused or lost.

A missing book must be replaced."

"Of course," said Amelia Bedelia.

"Rules are rules," said Mrs. Page.

"You have to go by the book."

"Right," said Amelia Bedelia.

"We have to go buy the book."

"You see," said Mrs. Page,

"lots of people depend on us,

especially those

who cannot visit the library.

I mean, take our bookmobile . . ."

An assistant interrupted her.

"Oh, Mrs. Page, the head librarian

will be here in twenty minutes."

"Goodness," said Mrs. Page.

She ran off to get ready.

"Lisa," said Amelia Bedelia,

"Mrs. Page told us what to do.

We need to go buy the book.

And we can take the bookmobile."

"May I come, too?" said Lisa.

"Sure," said Amelia Bedelia.

"Just ask your mother first."

"Here she comes," said Lisa.

"She was teaching an art class."

Lisa's mom gave permission.

"May I ask a favor?"

said Amelia Bedelia.

"These children may need help

with bookmarks and reports."

"I'd be glad to help," Lisa's mom said.

"Thanks," said Amelia Bedelia.

"We'll be right back."

"I love this bookmobile,"

said Lisa.

"Me, too," said Amelia Bedelia.

"Let's pretend we have checked out

all these books for ourselves."

"Lucky us," said Lisa.

"It was nice of Mrs. Page

to loan us the bookmobile,"

said Lisa.

"It was all her idea,"

said Amelia Bedelia.

"Stay here, Sam," said Lisa.

"And stay away from the books."

"I found the book," said Amelia Bedelia.

"Good work," said Lisa.

"Guess what I found? A thesaurus."

"Where is it?" asked Amelia Bedelia.

"Right behind you," said Lisa.

"Run! Hide!" said Amelia Bedelia.

Lisa laughed out loud.

"Come back," she said.

"A thesaurus is not

a dinosaur, after all."

"Jeepers," said Amelia Bedelia.

"Look at all these words.

I can find just the right one to use."

A man walked up to them.

"I am the manager of this store.

What is all the ruckus about?"

"Ruckus?" said Amelia Bedelia.

"I like that word. Let's look it up.

I would love to use it in a story."

"Ah-hah," said the manager.

"Follow me. You are late."

"I am?" said Amelia Bedelia.

He led them straight to the

children's section of the bookstore.

He said, "I like your costume.

I have never met a storyteller

who dresses like a housekeeper."

Lisa laughed.

Amelia Bedelia did not laugh.

She did not want to disappoint

the manager or the children.

Amelia Bedelia told a terrific story

about dinosaurs attacking the library.

Mrs. Page, the brave librarian,

saved every book from being chomped.

"All in all, it was quite a ruckus,"

said Amelia Bedelia.

"You are great,"

said the children.

"You are talented,"

said the manager.

"You are in trouble,"

said a police officer.

"What's wrong?" said the manager.

"There must be some mistake."

"There sure is," said the officer.

"This lady took that bookmobile."

"I sure did," said Amelia Bedelia.

"Mrs. Page told me to."

"Don't worry,"

said the officer.

"They won't throw

the book at you."

"I hope not,"

said Amelia Bedelia.

"I just bought it."

The officer smiled.

"I will trust you to drive

back to the library,"

she said.

They returned the bookmobile.

"I wonder if Mrs. Page is upset,"

said Amelia Bedelia.

"Why would she be upset?"

said Lisa. "We bought the book."

Mrs. Page was not smiling.

Neither was the woman

standing beside her.

"I owe you an apology,"

said Amelia Bedelia.

"Sam had ruined a book.

You said, 'Go buy the book.'

So we borrowed the bookmobile

and bought the book."

"Oh, dear," said Mrs. Page.

"What happened to our book?

 Were the pages torn or just dog-eared?"

"Ask Sam," said Amelia Bedelia.

"He's still digesting it."

"Hey, there! Welcome back,"

said Lisa's mom.

"I know some other creatures

who would like to say hello."

ARRRRGH!

"I am the word-eating Thesaurus!

If you need a better word,

look inside me!"

"I am the Flying Periodical.

I buzz by every week!"

"I am the Giant Prehistoric Bookworm!

If I had a nose, it would be in a book."

The woman who had not smiled

was now laughing.

"You are all amazing," she said.

"I have been the head librarian

for twenty years,

but I have never seen children

have such fun with books."

"Lisa's mom helped everyone,"

said Amelia Bedelia.

"So you are the head librarian.

I have heard all about you.

You are the know-it-all

who has been around forever."

Mrs. Page was about to faint.

The woman laughed and said,

"I guess I am a dinosaur."

"Let's check," said Amelia Bedelia.

"Is your last name Saurus?"

"No," she said, "it is Cramer."

"I am sorry," said Amelia Bedelia.

"You cannot be a dinosaur."

"What a relief," said Mrs. Cramer.

"There is a big parade next week,"

Mrs. Cramer said.

"Would you all march for the library?"

On the day of the parade

Amelia Bedelia stopped by the library.

"Amelia Bedelia," said Mrs. Page,

"I *am* glad to see you.

Come see what Mark made for you."

Amelia Bedelia looked up

at the ceiling.

"Is that a mobile?"

"It is a *book* mobile," said Mrs. Page.

"How sweet," said Amelia Bedelia.

"Just remember," said Mrs. Page.

"You can borrow the books

but not the bookmobile."

They laughed.

Then they went out together

to watch the parade.

Amelia Bedelia, Rocket Scientist?

BY HERMAN PARISH

PICTURES BY LYNN SWEAT

Greenwillow Books

An Imprint of HarperCollins*Publishers*

For Philip,
the original "Happy Man"—H. P.

To my sisters,
Evelyn and Betty—L. S.

"**T**his is incredible," said Mr. Rogers.

"Who is the rocket scientist

who put my glasses in the dishwasher?"

"I am," said Amelia Bedelia.

"Thank you for promoting me.

You told me to wash all of the glasses."

"Wait just a minute," said Mr. Rogers.

"Reading glasses are different."

"Sorry," said Amelia Bedelia,

"I cannot wait a second.

Miss Edwards, the science teacher,

needs my help at the science fair."

"Science?" said Mr. Rogers.

"You don't know anything about science."

Amelia Bedelia was too far away to hear.

"Wait," he called out. "You forgot your—"

135

Amelia Bedelia arrived at the school.

"Mr. Rogers is so thoughtful,"

she said to herself.

"He promoted me from housekeeper

to rocket scientist

just in time for the science fair."

SCIENCE
★ FAIR ★
TODAY

SCHOOL

"Wow," said Amelia Bedelia.

"Look at all these amazing projects.

Miss Edwards makes science

such fun."

"Hi, Miss Edwards," said Amelia Bedelia.

"Happy science fair."

"Same to you," said Miss Edwards.

"I'm so glad you volunteered to help."

"Sorry I am late," said Amelia Bedelia.

"Mr. Rogers called my work incredible,

and then he promoted me."

"Congratulations," said Miss Edwards.

"I just got here, too. I was in a make-up test."

"You should get an A," said Amelia Bedelia.

"Your lipstick looks great."

"It was not for me," said Miss Edwards.

"The make-up test was for my students."

"Are you kidding?" said Amelia Bedelia.

"These children are way too young

to wear makeup."

"I agree," said Miss Edwards.

"The only things they had to make up

were the answers."

"What a big kid!" said Amelia Bedelia.

"He is a judge," said Miss Edwards.

"A judge?" said Amelia Bedelia.

"Shouldn't he be in court?"

"Not quite," said Miss Edwards.

"He is judging our science fair.

He is a famous scientist.

I invited him from the university."

"Amelia Bedelia," said Miss Edwards,

"I would like you to meet Dr. Dinglebatt."

"Hello there," said the man.

"I am Don Dinglebatt, professor."

"Pleased to meet you," said Amelia Bedelia.

"I am Amelia Bedelia, rocket scientist."

"Oh, really?" said Dr. Dinglebatt.

"Yes, really," said Amelia Bedelia.

"I also keep house for Mrs. Rogers."

"Housekeeping?" said Dr. Dinglebatt.

"You call that rocket science?"

"Not me," said Amelia Bedelia.

"That's what Mr. Rogers calls it."

"Good for you," said Dr. Dinglebatt.

"It sounds like Mr. Rogers

respects the work you do."

"Yes," said Miss Edwards.

"And your job, Dr. Dinglebatt,

is to judge every science project."

"Yes, indeed," said Dr. Dinglebatt.

"When I see the winner

I will shout 'Eureka!'"

"What is a eureka?" said Amelia Bedelia.

Miss Edwards shrugged and said,

"It is Greek to me."

"It is Greek to everyone,"

said Dr. Dinglebatt.

"In ancient Greece, a famous scientist

named Archimedes shouted 'Eureka!'

when he made a discovery in the bath."

"I get it," said Amelia Bedelia.

"*Eureka* means 'Ouch, this water is hot!'"

"No, it doesn't," said Dr. Dinglebatt.

"*Eureka* means 'I have found it.'"

"Found what?" asked Miss Edwards.

"The soap," said Amelia Bedelia.

"No, no, no!" said Dr. Dinglebatt.

"It means 'I found the answer.'"

A boy interrupted them.

"Excuse me," said Jason.

"I wanted to let you know that

a volcano will erupt in ten minutes."

"Take cover!" yelled Amelia Bedelia.

Jason laughed and said,

"Relax, this volcano is just a model."

"Is it safe now?"

said Amelia Bedelia.

"All clear," said Miss Edwards.

"I am glad to see that you take

this science fair so seriously.

You can assist Dr. Dinglebatt.

Right now I have to help Emily

set up her homemade telescope."

"Okay, Jason," said Dr. Dinglebatt.

"Let's test-drive your volcano."

They did not get very far.

"Hey, Jason," said Wendy.

"Would you help me get my saucer?

I hooked up my dad's leaf blower

to show how a flying saucer flies."

FLYING SAUCERS

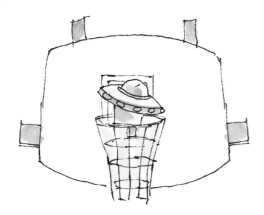

"Where is the cup?" said Amelia Bedelia.

"Flying saucers do not come

with their own teacups," said Dr. Dinglebatt.

"I see," said Amelia Bedelia,

"but I don't see a saucer."

"It is stuck up there,"

said Wendy.

"What a shame," said Amelia Bedelia.

"Would my bonnet work instead?"

"It might," said Wendy.

"Give it a try," said Dr. Dinglebatt.

"You are the rocket scientist."

Amelia Bedelia counted down:

"Five, four, three, two, one . . . blastoff!"

Wendy turned on the blower.

WHIR-R-R-R-RRR

Up, up, up went the bonnet.

"We have liftoff!" said Dr. Dinglebatt.

As Amelia Bedelia moved the blower,

her bonnet flew around and around.

On the other side of the gym,

Emily shouted, "Look! It's a UFO!"

Miss Edwards focused the telescope.

"No, it isn't," she said.

"That flying object

is not unidentified.

It belongs to Amelia Bedelia.

I must go see what's going on."

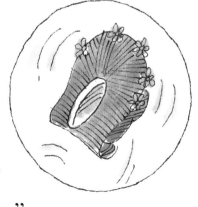

"This is great," said Amelia Bedelia.

"It isn't scientific," said Dr. Dinglebatt.

"What fun," said Amelia Bedelia.

"UFOs don't exist," said Dr. Dinglebatt.

"Wheeeee!" said Amelia Bedelia.

"I am the judge," said Dr. Dinglebatt.

"I deserve a turn . . .

uh, I mean, to test it."

Dr. Dinglebatt reached for the blower.

He turned it off by mistake.

Amelia Bedelia's bonnet fell to earth.

"Look out below," said Amelia Bedelia.

"I had better get my bonnet

before it becomes another project."

She ran over to the next aisle.

155

"Eureka!" shouted Amelia Bedelia.

Dr. Dinglebatt came running.

"What is it?" he said.

"Did you find a winner?"

"No," said Amelia Bedelia.

"I found my bonnet.

Look where it landed!"

"A fellow housekeeper," said Dr. Dinglebatt.

"What a neat robot," said Amelia Bedelia.

"That is the whole idea," said Artie.

"My mom wants my room to be neat."

"Your mother is right," said Dr. Dinglebatt.

"I know," said Artie. "She always says,

'Pick up your room, pick up your room!'"

"That is impossible," said Amelia Bedelia.

"Your room must weigh a ton!

You could never pick up the bed,

the rug, the desk . . ."

"I believe," said Dr. Dinglebatt,

"that Artie's mother wants him

to pick up all the things on his floor:

his toys, his books, his clothes . . ."

"Oh, I see," said Amelia Bedelia.

"No wonder you are a professor."

Dr. Dinglebatt smiled and said,

"Okay, Artie, let's see Randy in action."

"Here is how he works," said Artie.

"I put little pieces of metal on all my stuff.

Then I put magnets on my robot's hands."

"So," continued Artie, "if I leave my stuff

on the floor, I can turn on Randy . . ."

"Presto—all picked up.

 My mom is happy."

"Bravo!" said Dr. Dinglebatt.

"You are a first-rate inventor."

"Thanks," said Artie.

"Randy still has a few bugs in him."

"I can fix that," said Amelia Bedelia.

"Shoo!" said Amelia Bedelia.

"I'm warning you bugs.

Get out of Randy right now."

"Be careful," joked Dr. Dinglebatt.

"That contraption might replace you.

Imagine an army of housekeeping robots."

"That is scary," said Amelia Bedelia.

"Yoo-hoo," Miss Edwards called out.

Amelia Bedelia jumped.

"Hey," said Amelia Bedelia,

"don't scare me like that."

"Well, well," said Miss Edwards.

"I was worried that you two

might not be getting along."

"We get along fine,"

said Dr. Dinglebatt.

"So I see,"

said Miss Edwards.

YIPES!

163

"Look at the time," said Amelia Bedelia.

"We don't want to miss the volcano."

"I'm afraid I will," said Miss Edwards.

"Emily and her telescope still need help."

"See you later?" said Dr. Dinglebatt.

Miss Edwards just walked away.

"I think she is mad," said Dr. Dinglebatt.

"I don't blame her," said Amelia Bedelia.

"I would hate to miss an erupting volcano."

"I'll meet you there," said Dr. Dinglebatt.

"I need to look at some other projects."

"Hi, Jason," said Amelia Bedelia.

"When does your volcano erupt?"

"Never," said Jason.

"I have run out of baking soda."

Amelia Bedelia reached into her purse.

"You are in luck," said Amelia Bedelia.

"I just did a lot of baking.

I bought an extra box at the store."

"Oh, thank you, thank you," said Jason.

"One day I will win the Nobel Prize."

"Why no bell?" said Amelia Bedelia.

"Do they give buzzers instead?"

"No," said Jason. "The Nobel Prize

is the most important award in science."

"I hope you win it," said Amelia Bedelia.

"Show me how your volcano works."

"Step one," said Jason.

"Add a little bit of baking soda . . .

Step two: add some vinegar . . .

Uh-oh. I ran out of that, too."

"I can't help you,"

said Amelia Bedelia.

"Maybe the cafeteria

can spare some vinegar."

"Good idea," said Jason.

"I'll be right back."

"This volcano is amazing,"

said Amelia Bedelia to herself.

"Jason worked so hard on his project.

I hope Dr. Dinglebatt is impressed, too."

Amelia Bedelia had an idea.

She poured the rest of the baking soda

into the volcano.

"Saved again," said Jason.

"A nice cafeteria lady

loaned me some vinegar."

Just then Dr. Dinglebatt arrived.

"Looks like I am just in time," he said.

"You sure are," said Jason.

"Would you pour in the vinegar?"

"Sure," said Dr. Dinglebatt.

"It would be an honor."

The lava began to bubble.

Jason put on the top.

"Watch this," he said.

The volcano rumbled loudly.

"Is that normal?" said Wendy.

The volcano rocked and rolled.

"Is something wrong?" said Artie.

"Hmmm," said Amelia Bedelia.

"Maybe I should not have dumped in

that whole box of baking soda."

"A whole box?" said Dr. Dinglebatt.

"Run!" yelled Jason. "It's about to—"

"Gangway!" said Amelia Bedelia.

"This blower will blow it away."

WHIR-R-R-R

went the blower.

WHOOOOSH went

Dr. Dinglebatt's hair.

Miss Edwards heard the commotion

from across the gym.

She looked through the telescope.

"Gracious," said Miss Edwards.

"Now *that* is a UFO.

I'd better get over there."

"My hair!" said Dr. Dinglebatt.

The children pointed and laughed.

Amelia Bedelia turned off the blower.

The hairpiece fell back to earth.

"Eeeeek!" screamed a girl.

"A rat is attacking the mouse!"

Dr. Dinglebatt scooped up his hair.

"Excuse me, young lady," he said.

"This rat is going back to my lab."

Eeeeek!

Amelia Bedelia was just as upset.

"It's all my fault," she said.

"I was trying to help Jason

win the Nobel Prize."

"Nobel Prize?" said Dr. Dinglebatt.

"This deserves the dumbbell prize!"

Dr. Dinglebatt stalked out of the gym.

"He is a mad scientist," said Jason.

"You mean he is crazy?" said Artie.

"Like you see in horror movies?"

"No," said Wendy. "He is angry."

"He sure is," said Amelia Bedelia.

"When he found his hair,

he forgot to say 'Eureka!'"

"What happened?" said Miss Edwards.

Amelia Bedelia explained everything.

"How embarrassing," said Miss Edwards.

"Dr. Dinglebatt had a bad hair day."

"Worse than that," said Amelia Bedelia,

"he had a no hair day."

"Worst of all," said Miss Edwards.

"Our science fair has no winner."

"I feel terrible," said Amelia Bedelia.

"I ruined Jason's project.

I embarrassed Dr. Dinglebatt.

I don't feel like a rocket scientist.

I am going back to housekeeping."

Amelia Bedelia picked up a broom.

Everyone helped clean up the mess.

Even Randy the Robot was lending a claw.

"Amelia Bedelia," said Miss Edwards.

"Do not be so hard on yourself.

Many scientific breakthroughs

are made by accidents and mistakes."

"In that case," said Amelia Bedelia,

"I should get two Nobel Prizes:

one for blowing the volcano's top,

and one for blowing Dr. Dinglebatt's top."

They had just finished cleaning up

when the gym door flew open.

"Eureka!" shouted Dr. Dinglebatt.

"I found it, I found it!"

"I take it back," said Amelia Bedelia.

"He is happy he found his hair."

"Are you still a mad scientist?"

   asked Artie.

"Mad?" said Dr. Dinglebatt.

"I am not a mad man.

   I am a happy man!"

"That's a switch,"

   said Miss Edwards.

"Precisely," said Dr. Dinglebatt.

"Back at my lab, I was inspired

   to improve my latest invention.

   I switched a switch,

   added a little surprise,

   and here it is."

"We've got one of those," said Jason.

"It is a TV remote control."

"That's right," said Dr. Dinglebatt.

"But this remote control can never get lost."

"My dad needs one of those," said Artie.

"Everyone does," said Wendy.

"How does it work?"

"Clap your hands," said Dr. Dinglebatt.

"Look familiar?" said Dr. Dinglebatt.

"I call it my Tip-Top Remote.

It blows its top before you blow yours!

And I am giving half of the credit to a

rocket scientist named Amelia Bedelia."

"That is terrific," said Miss Edwards.

"Thanks for coming back to show us."

"Actually," said Dr. Dinglebatt,

"I came back to apologize.

I am sorry I lost my temper."

"No harm done," said Amelia Bedelia.

"I am glad," said Dr. Dinglebatt.

"In fact, I will recommend

that my university

sponsor your fair from now on."

"Hooray," shouted the children.

"Wonderful," said Miss Edwards.

They were still clapping and cheering

when Mr. Rogers walked in.

"Thank you!" said Mr. Rogers.

"It is nice to feel appreciated."

"Stop dreaming," said Amelia Bedelia.

"We are not clapping for you."

"You should," said Mr. Rogers.

"I brought in your science project."

"My what?" said Amelia Bedelia.

"Don't be modest," said Miss Edwards.

"Aha!" said Dr. Dinglebatt.

"You really are a rocket scientist."

"No," said Mr. Rogers. "I was wrong.

Amelia Bedelia is actually a chemist."

"I am?" said Amelia Bedelia.

"You bet," said Mr. Rogers.

"Here is her secret formula:

Combine citric acid, H_2O, cornstarch,

sucrose, and a pinch of sodium chloride.

Pour it into a pan lined with ground wheat.

Cover with protein. Heat to 350 degrees.

When the top turns brown, it's done."

"That is incredible," said Miss Edwards.

"Sounds edible," said Dr. Dinglebatt.

"I sure hope so," said Amelia Bedelia.

"It is my recipe for lemon meringue pie.

I made pies for my fellow scientists."

"And here they are," said Mr. Rogers.

"You left these pies behind this morning."

"Amelia Bedelia," said Dr. Dinglebatt,

"you are an amazing cook."

"Amazing what?" said Amelia Bedelia.

"I mean," said Dr. Dinglebatt,

"you are an amazing chemist.

I have just one word for your pie."

said Mr. Rogers.

said Miss Edwards.

said Amelia Bedelia.

Dr. Dinglebatt pointed at his pie

and shouted: "Eureka!"